The nine lives of Oscar the cat

Contents

This book is dedicated to my family and friends
for their enthusiasm and encouragement,
especially Martin for his absolute belief I could
do it and of course to a little cat called Oscar,
the purr-fect inspiration.

Chapter 1

In a spin

"All cats have nine lives," that's what Oscar's mum says and she's never wrong. The problem was, Oscar was down to his last life if that was true.

Oscar was a black and white cat with white paws and tummy. He had a black smudge round his right eye that looked just like a number nine and his mum said that was to remind him how many lives he had. His big green eyes were always full of mischief and although he was smaller than your average cat, what he lacked in stature, he made up for in scrapes. Oscar was always getting into scrapes, "lucky escapes" his mum called them, but like most cats he always landed on his feet.

Sally, Oscar's mum, had a saying:

"Four paws on the ground, safe and sound; four paws in the air, don't go there" and she's never wrong!

When Oscar was born, with all nine lives still intact, nobody thought he'd be the one to get into so much trouble. As a young kitten, he would always do what his mum said and rarely ventured out of the spare room. As he grew older though, his kitten curiosity led him further afield and this is where his first adventure started, and his first life was lost.

It was a sunny Saturday morning, Oscar yawned, opened his eyes and decided he was bored of the spare room. Sally was stretched out on the windowsill snoozing, her pure grey fur almost blue in the light. His two older sisters, Susie and Sophie were sound asleep too. Susie was the bigger of the two, round with the thickest fur of silver, white and brown stripes; she was easygoing, never in a hurry and loved to sleep more than any cat Oscar had ever met. 'Snoozy Susie' Mr Martin would call her and it suited her well.

Sophie was totally different. She was dainty and delicate looking; she never broke the rules and was scared of everything. She was a silver tabby and always kept her fur in tip-top condition with constant grooming. Oscar didn't look like either of them.

Another thing that had also puzzled Oscar was his name. It was a Martin family tradition that all pets be called something starting with the letter "S". It had all started with Bella, Sally and Oscar's human owner. She was ten and loved all things that started with "S": seaside, sandcastles, sweets, sunflowers, swings, sleepovers. Her first pet was a goldfish called Solo who she won at the local fair, then came Snowy the white rabbit, Smarty the hamster and then Sally, Sophie and Susie.

Oscar was from a litter of four kittens. Bella wanted to keep them all, but her mum and dad insisted she would have to give them away. Oscar's three brothers were found new homes easily; they were big and strong and didn't mind leaving Sally at all. When it came time for Oscar to leave, a man in a holey jumper and dirty jeans turned up and tried to shove Oscar into a small wire cage. Oscar panicked, hissing and spitting, fighting like a wild cat. When the man tried to catch him, Oscar scratched him on the nose, the man let go and ran for the door, never to return. From that day Mr Martin nicknamed him "Oscar Wilde Cat" after a famous playwright and said he could stay. Bella sometimes secretly called him "Soscar", but he didn't mind too much because he knew how much she loved the letter "S", so much in fact that she gave him his favourite treat on Saturdays - sardines.

This Saturday, Oscar had eaten his bowl of sardines and was now bored. He was tired of staying in the spare room and wanted to explore. Feeling brave, he pushed his nose on the bedroom door which opened just enough for him to squeeze through.

Once on the landing, Oscar had a decision to make. All the doors around him were closed and the landing looked as dull and boring as the room he'd just come from. The Martin family lived in a large old house with a steep spiral staircase that led from the attic landing down to the second floor. Oscar had never been down spiral stairs before and wasn't quite sure how to do it. Gingerly he took his first step. The wrought iron was cold under his paws, but he kept on going. One step at a time, round and round, down and down. Eventually he reached the bottom, rather dizzy, but excited by the start of his adventure. The stairs down to the ground floor were easy in comparison and Oscar virtually flew down them, skidding on the polished floor and sliding half way down the hall.

"Brilliant," thought Oscar. "I can't wait to do that again, that was so much fun."

Everything smelt familiar, yet different. A coat on a stand in the hall smelt like Bella, clean and lovely, but then he smelt something horrible, one of Bella's dad's running shoes.

"Pooh," thought Oscar.

He jumped onto the sofa, along the back and onto a shelf, and that's when he saw it: a small black and white cat staring straight at him. Oscar was quite scared as he didn't know who this intruder was, but he decided to be brave. He fluffed up his fur and hissed...and the other cat did the same.

"Now what?" thought Oscar. "If I back down, he'll think I'm a wussy cat."

Oscar spiked up his coat even more and crept forward, never taking his eyes off the other cat. It started to edge forward too.

Oscar lashed out with his paw and *whack*, he hit something cold and hard. He'd been ready to fight a mirror! Now he felt very silly. His mum had told him about "copy cats" and how our reflections do everything we do, but this was the first one he'd ever seen. He now had a good look and decided his copy cat was actually quite handsome and not scary at all. He left the copy cat alone and went to explore the other exciting places.

Over to the rug for a quick scratch to check his claws were in tip top condition, then onto the rocking chair....whoah...... off the rocking chair, through the double doors and into the kitchen.

Oscar stopped to have a good look round. The kitchen smelt different to the other rooms, a strange mixture of yummy food smells and yucky disinfectant. The floor felt strange under his paws. Slippery and smooth, cold and uncomfortable. He jumped into the air and landed with a graceful thud on the kitchen worktop.

A pan was bubbling away on the stove, but Oscar had never seen one before and didn't realise it could be dangerous. He soon found out. Sniffing the contents of the pan (*yuck* – boiled cabbage) he wrinkled up his nose and turned to walk away in disgust. As he turned, his tail swished and caught the pan handle and before Oscar knew what was happening, there was a huge clatter and the cabbage was all over the clean kitchen floor.

"Uh oh," thought Oscar. "I'm in BIG trouble now." He could hear footsteps running down the stairs, closer and closer. Mrs Martin would be in any second and Oscar had to act fast.

Quickly he leapt off the worktop, but his front right paw caught the draining board and knocked one of the drying dishes. It was like watching dominoes fall in slow motion, as one by one the dishes started their descent. Oscar dodged a huge dinner plate, but slicing through the air towards him was a carving knife. Its blade was shiny and sharp, the pointed end aiming right for him. He turned, but too late, the knife caught his paw, the one that started all the trouble in the first place.

"Owwwwww!" meowed Oscar. "That hurts."

As he looked down to inspect the damage, he saw a bright red trickle of blood where the blade had caught him.

Mrs Martin was in the lounge now, running towards the kitchen. Oscar was frightened and needed a hiding place, but where? Then he saw it. A hole behind a round door, open just a crack. He wasn't sure if he could squeeze in, but he managed to, just as Mrs Martin came in to see the devastation.

"What on earth has happened here?" Mrs Martin was looking very confused and rather red in the face. Quiet as a mouse, Oscar stayed put. His paw hurt and he started to feel faint and very tired. He couldn't keep his eyes open.

"Bella!" shouted Mrs Martin up the stairs. "Can you come downstairs and help me tidy up this mess please?"

Bella skipped into the kitchen and stopped suddenly when she saw all the cabbage and broken dishes on the floor.

"What's happened Mum?"

"I have no idea, but we're going to visit Grandma shortly and I haven't even managed to put the washing in yet."

"No problem, I'll help."

Bella went back upstairs, emptied the laundry basket on the landing and then picked up a heap of white shirts and socks.

Oscar was dreaming. He was chasing a mouse. It was big, brown and rather ugly, but surprisingly fast. The mouse stopped at a big puddle and Oscar jumped to get him, but as he did, he saw the water rise up into a huge wave. Oscar hated water, but the wave came after him and crashed down on his head. He spluttered. He was wet, soaking wet. Startled, he woke up. He was chest deep in soapy water and the ground was moving.

Oscar was now very scared and let out a loud meow, but water poured into his mouth and he was losing his balance. Things were getting tangled in his paws, he started to panic, but the more he struggled, the worse it got. Soap was stinging his eyes, his paw was bleeding, turning the water red and he couldn't breathe. He was terrified and had no idea how to escape.

Bella was helping her mum clean up the cabbage splattered floor when she saw something odd. The washing machine didn't look quite right. She'd been really careful to put only white things in, but she could see something black. She pressed her nose to the thick glass, trying to make out what it was and then screamed.

"Mum, Mum – we have to stop the machine. I think one of the kittens has gotten in!"

Mrs Martin took one look at Bella's ashen face and knew she wasn't making it up. She could also see what looked like a tiny paw and a tip of a tail. Bella felt sick and tears were streaming down her face. Mrs Martin was trying to stay calm and tugged at the wire to unplug the machine.

She grabbed a screwdriver from the drawer and with all her strength prised open the door. Water came gushing out all over the kitchen floor and there, wrapped in one of Bella's soggy school shirts with a sock over one eye, was Oscar. Wet, bedraggled, shocked, paw still bleeding, but generally okay. Bella scooped him up and squeezed him, so glad that they found him before it was too late.

A few hours later and Oscar was tucked up next to his sisters in the spare room. He felt alright now but he knew he'd had a lucky escape. Sally was both upset and angry and said he wasn't to leave the room again without asking permission.

She spent the next hour grooming him, to try and get his fur back to normal. It was then that she noticed the tell-tale sign. A strange grey hair that refused to lie flat. She told Oscar he had used up one of his nine lives and the wiry grey hair was a permanent reminder that his nine lives had become eight.

In his next adventure, why did the cat cross the road? To prove he is so strong and bold.

Chapter 2

Look both ways

It was a warm Sunday afternoon when Sally told the kittens that she was going to teach them some very important things, things that could save their lives. Oscar wondered if his mum was a black belt in karate or a secret agent for the government. He was looking forward to learning how to disarm an opponent at twenty paces or how to use the Meow code (similar to the human Morse code, but using meows and mews instead.) What Sally had planned was far more important than any secret mission; she wanted to teach the kittens...The Green Cross Code.

"Awww Mum, that's SO boring," said Oscar. "Everyone knows how to cross the road."

"Oh really," replied Sally with a hint of amusement in her voice. "Would you like to explain to your sisters then?"

Sophie pulled a face as Oscar tried to think what he had heard Mrs Martin tell Bella.

"You stop, look and listen and only cross when it's safe," said Oscar with an air of authority.

"Well done Oscar, that's exactly what you should do, and now we're going to put it into practice." Sally told the kittens to follow her and to do exactly what she said.

Oscar took the lead, Sophie in the middle and Susie brought up the rear. Sally leapt gracefully out of the landing window and onto the conservatory roof.

Oscar was a confident jumper and landed quite easily next to his mum. Sophie was next and although a bit unsure at first, "Scaredy Cat" comments from Oscar ensured that she was on the roof in no time. The problem was Susie. Although bigger and stronger than Oscar and Sophie, she really disliked any kind of exercise. The very thought of leaping on the roof had worn her out and she was ready for a catnap.

"Come on Susie, we'll only be out a short while and then you can get back to your basket." Sally was having no nonsense and wanted all the kittens to join in.

"But I'm tired," Susie let out a yawn. "Can't I do it another day? Please?"

"No Susie, you will join us right this minute or I'll be confiscating your basket and you'll have to sleep on the floor!" Sally knew how to push the right buttons and reluctantly, Susie jumped down and landed with a large thud on the roof. The cats then walked in convoy along the roof, onto the fence, into the garden and round the pond.

"Wow!" said Oscar. "What are those, Mum?"

Oscar was staring into the garden pond and watching the strange orange and gold shapes moving about in the water.

"Those are fish. Koi carp to be precise. Mr Martin is very proud of them, so don't touch."

"Ooh, they're really pretty Mum," said Sophie as she edged forward for a closer look. She dipped her paw towards the water, but was stopped by Sally meowing loudly at her.

"I said, no touching!"

Sophie quickly pulled her paw back, "Sorry Mum."

They followed Sally out of the garden and into a nearby cul-de-sac. "OK, here we are. Everyone stay put." Sally had brought them to the edge of a cobbled road, but it didn't lead anywhere and there were no cars to be seen.

"Mum, why are we here?" Oscar asked.

"I want you to meet someone and then we can practise." Sally let out a loud meow and seconds later a big black head with green eyes appeared over the fence.

"Hi Max, thanks for coming, I hope we haven't disturbed your afternoon nap."

"Not at all, always a pleasure. I was wondering when I'd get to meet the little ones."

Oscar puffed up his coat in indignation. He wasn't little, although, actually, when he compared himself to Max, he realised he was. Max was massive. He was like the panthers Bella watched on the television. Completely black, sleek and with more than a few battle scars, Max had certainly been a fighter in his day.

And then Oscar noticed something rather odd. He counted again. One, two, three? Where was number four? Max caught Oscar looking at him, his head cocked to one side in deep concentration.

"You can look all you like, you won't find it," said Max with amusement.

Oscar blushed, and then couldn't help but ask the obvious.

"Sorry to stare, but where's your leg gone?"

Max was missing his left back leg. In its place was a stump and his tail waved to help with his balance.

"Now that, I imagine, is why your mum has brought you all to see me," Max wiggled his stump for full effect.

All the kittens looked in horror. Sophie started to cry, Susie keeled over and Oscar was rooted to the spot, staring at the place where Max's leg should be.

"Sophie, why are you crying, Max is okay," Sally asked with concern.

"I like...all my...legs...I...don't...want...to...lose one," she replied between sobs.

"Don't be so silly Sophie, Max isn't going to chop off your leg! He's going to tell you how it happened, so you can learn from his mistake."

Sophie stopped sobbing and Susie got up from where she had fainted.

"What happened?" she yawned.

"Max is going to tell us how he got his leg chopped off!" Oscar said excitedly.

Max ran over to the kittens, he was surprisingly agile and his missing limb didn't slow him down at all.

"Now, where shall I start?" Max sat down and the kittens did the same, lapping up his every word.

Max told his story in less than five minutes, but it would stay with the kittens for a long time to come. Two years ago he had been living on the streets with a gang of stray cats called the Shadows. He was the leader and the other cats always looked up to him.

One night, he was patrolling his patch near the pizza shop, when he saw a cat from a rival gang, a nasty flea-ridden Tom called Ginger. Max had heard Ginger had been bullying other cats in the area and generally causing trouble.

Ginger spotted him and hissed from across the road, swiping his claws in the air, ready for battle. Max knew Ginger fought dirty and fixed his eye on his opponent. He stepped into the road, hackles raised, ready for action.

Determined to defend his territory, he didn't notice the car. It was travelling fast toward him, and when he looked up, it was too late. Bam! His back leg was caught under the wheel.

The kittens all flinched as Max told his true life horror story. He told them he blacked out and when he came round, he was wrapped in a blanket, in a strange room and his leg was gone.

Liz the girl from the pizza shop had seen what had happened and had rushed him to an emergency vet. Unfortunately his leg was too badly damaged to save and they had to amputate it. Liz then brought him home and he'd lived there ever since.

"Wow," Oscar was in awe. "But what happened to the Shadows?"

Max looked wistful for a moment. "I still see them occasionally, but some of them think I sold out by coming to live here. House cats were always looked down on to be honest. Having regular meals, a warm place to sleep and an owner who loves me isn't that bad really."

Oscar thought about Bella and Mr and Mrs Martin. He loved nothing better than curling up with Bella on the sofa, his head on her lap as she tickled his chin. Being a house cat was great, he got sardines on Saturdays and even Mr Martin would play with him with a bit of string when he thought no-one was looking. Oscar thought the Shadows had it all wrong.

Sally thanked Max and he disappeared back over the fence as she ushered the kittens round the corner towards the road.

"OK, are we all ready to cross over safely?" Sally spent the next twenty minutes practising road safety with the kittens who were now much more interested in doing it properly.

Later that evening, Oscar was sprawled out on the big red chair in the lounge thinking about Max and his story. He was just about to have a catnap when he overheard Bella and her Mum talking.

"I was hissed at by a cat today Mum."

"Not one of ours I hope?" Mrs Martin disliked bad manners in people and pets.

"No, it was a big ginger one by the pizza shop. I went over to stroke it and he hissed at me. He looked quite angry."

Oscar's ears pricked up. That sounded like Ginger, the Tom cat that Max had told them about. If he was hanging out by the pizza shop again, Max might be in trouble.

Oscar needed a plan. He liked Max and wanted to help, but knew his Mum wouldn't let him go out on his own. He didn't want to get into trouble, but he felt it was his duty to warn Max about Ginger. Oscar was going to have to sneak out when no-one was looking.

The downstairs utility window was open a crack, just big enough for Oscar to squeeze through. The evening air was crisp and cool, Oscar could feel his heart pumping fast but he had to be brave and find Max to warn him.

It took Oscar twenty minutes to find the pizza shop, he could smell lots of different flavours all mixed together: ham, tuna, chicken, but he couldn't see Max anywhere.

He looked down the alley where all the big dustbins were kept, but there was no sign of him. He looked in the bus shelter with the graffiti and cracked glass. He wasn't there. He was just about to give up and go home when he heard a loud meow coming from the alley. He looked down the dimly lit street and saw two bright orange eyes peering from the top of one of the bins.

"Max?" Oscar called out, uncertain what to do." Is that you Max?"

"Who's there?" snarled a deep, rough, unfamiliar voice.

Oscar was scared, but in his best grown up voice he said, "I'm looking for Max, have you seen him?"

"Max? You mean old Stumpy, the three-legged house cat? You won't see him out after dark anymore," the voice sneered.

The orange eyes moved out of the shadows into the dim light of a nearby lamp post and Oscar saw who the voice belonged to. The cat in front of him was big, but not like Max in a muscular way, more round and podgy with a huge head. His fur was un-groomed, a dirty ginger and white, and one of his ears had a chunk missing from it. Oscar realised who this was: Ginger the Tom cat he'd come to warn Max about.

"So, squirt, what are you doing out? It must be past your bed time. Why are you looking for Stumpy?" Ginger was edging closer and Oscar was starting to feel uncomfortable. "This is my patch and I don't take kindly to intruders on my turf. If you know what's good for you, I'd scat cat!"

Ginger narrowed his eyes and took another step towards him.

Oscar stood up as tall as he could. He didn't want Ginger to know how scared he was.

"I just want to see Max." He sounded braver than he felt.

"Well he isn't here kid. Just me and the gang patrolling the patch."

Two more pairs of eyes appeared from behind the dustbin. One cat was pale brown and scrawny, with thin legs and a pointy face; the other one had a long matted coat, a squashed face and a flat nose.

"Who's this boss?" said Scrawny.

"I don't know and I don't care. What I do know is that he's on our turf and that's tres-pawing." All three cats were now only a whisker away.

"Tell you what boys. Let's see if the kitty cat wants to play."

"Yeah boss, shall I find a squealer?" Scrawny ran round the bin and came back with a small, brown mouse in his mouth. The mouse looked terrified and was squirming to get away.

"At the count of three, let him go. First cat to catch the squealer gets the tuna head. Ready...one, two, three." Ginger leapt forward at the count of three and slammed his foot on the mouse's tail so he couldn't escape.

"Too slow boys." He flipped the fish head with his paw and caught it in his mouth. One gulp and it was gone. He lifted his foot and the mouse scurried towards the bin, but it was too late. Squash Face stood in its way and flicked him for fun with his paw. He skidded back towards Scrawny who promptly kicked him towards the pavement. The mouse was squealing with fear and was obviously confused.

"Stop it!" shouted Oscar. "You're hurting him!"

All three cats turned and stared at Oscar like they couldn't believe what they were hearing.

"What?" Ginger was sneering now, "The kitty cat doesn't want to play."

"Should we play fetch instead?" Squash Face was sniggering and Oscar didn't like the tone of his voice.

"Great idea...fetch!" Ginger picked up the mouse and flung him with all his force into the air. Higher and higher he went, then faster and faster he fell. Squash Face and Scrawny were both running wildly underneath, the mouse was twisting and turning mid-air desperate to escape from the captive claws beneath.

Scrawny caught him and leapt around with glee, then, remembering the game, threw the scared creature across the alley. He was hurtled towards Oscar, but he was too high and Oscar knew he would have to be quick to catch him. If the poor mouse landed on the floor, that would be the end of him. Oscar ran as fast as he could, and then leapt in the air and caught the mouse by the scruff of his neck.

Oscar landed with a thud on the road and then put the mouse down.

"Are you OK? Those cats are just horrible bullies." The little mouse was shaking, but nodded his head and ran off towards the bins. Oscar turned to face the bullies, angry that they had been so mean.

He was so focused on giving Ginger a piece of his mind that he didn't see the pizza delivery boy on his scooter until it was too late. Thud! margherita pizza all over the floor and Oscar was thrown into the air.

The next thing Oscar was aware of was a very bright light and the smell of antiseptic. The room was all white and a man with thick glasses and a mask was standing over him. Where was he?

He tried to stand up, but a sharp pain shot up his leg and he fell down again.

"Now puss, you need to rest that leg." The man had a warm, soothing voice. "You've had a nasty accident and broken a bone, so we need to set it." The man stroked Oscar under the chin and he felt much better.

Ten minutes later and Oscar had a pot on his leg and was wrapped in a warm blanket in the back of Mr Martin's car.

When Oscar arrived home, Bella was asleep in bed but had made him a "get well soon" card and put it by his food bowl, which was filled up with sardines. Sally was waiting in the attic room, her face a mixture of glad, sad and angry. Glad that Oscar was safe, sad he'd hurt his leg and angry he'd put himself in danger.

"You're going to need help getting washed while your leg heals." Sally couldn't stay angry at Oscar for long. She started to lick his head and as she groomed him, she found it. Another strange grey hair that wouldn't lay flat. Oscar had used up another of his lives, as nine became seven.

In his next adventure, Oscar makes a friend and meets a foe, but will his journey end in woe?

chapter 3

Bea and the bird

It was a lovely summer's day and Oscar was sat sunning himself on the patio by the fish pond. His leg had healed perfectly and he stretched it up above his head to demonstrate it was back in full working condition.

"Hey Soscar, you doing yoga again?"

Bella scooped him up and buried her face in his soft black fur. She walked towards the swing and sat down with Oscar draped over her shoulder like a furry scarf. Oscar loved the swing, it was one of his favourite things to do with Bella. He loved to feel the breeze through his whiskers and it felt as if he was flying.

Bella started to hum songs and Oscar could feel himself getting sleepy from the gentle rocking motion and her voice.

He crept down onto her knee, curled up and fell fast asleep. It was hours later when Oscar woke up on his own. Sometimes he would sleep for ages dreaming about chasing birds or eating sardines. This time he had dreamed he could fly like a bird and had been soaring over the rooftops and chimneys.

Oscar yawned, stood up, arched his back and stretched out. He felt great after his sleep and had lots of energy to use up. He perched on the garden bench to watch the fish for a while. He liked the way they moved and the flashes of colour in the water. He tried to strike up conversation with them, but every time he came close to the water's edge, the fish swam off in the opposite direction.

Then he heard a strange noise. It appeared to come from the rockery amongst the big purple flowers. He crept closer, curious to discover the source of the sound.

"Hello, is anyone there?" He couldn't see anyone, but it definitely sounded like there was someone close by.

"I'm over here." A little voice came from the direction of the biggest purple flower.

Oscar looked really hard, but couldn't see anyone.

"I'm here, on the flower."

Oscar looked closely and realised there was a tiny little bumblebee sat on the flower and her wing was bent at a funny angle.

"Are you OK?"

"My wing isn't working properly and I can't fly. I'm worried I won't be able to get home." The little bee looked sad as she tried to wiggle her wing.

Oscar wasn't sure what to do.

"Oh dear, would you like me to help you?" Oscar liked the bee and didn't want to see her looking so sad.

"Thank you, that's very kind, I'm quite tired now, I've been busy all day and the rest of the hive will be wondering where I am."

Oscar wasn't sure what a hive was, but was determined to help his new friend. He was curious about what she'd been doing all day and what she did with the pollen.

"I'll help you get home and if you're tired you can ride on my back if you want, if you promise not to sting me."

The little bee laughed, "You are obviously confusing me with a wasp. Bees don't sting you unless they are in real danger, wasps have no manners and do it for fun."

"What's a hive and what do you do with the pollen?" Oscar was curious about everything, his new friend was so very different from him.

"I'll show you if you want." She carefully climbed onto

Oscar's back and sat down. "Now we're friends, you can call me Beatrice, Bea for short."

Oscar and Bea started on their journey to Bluebell Woods. Oscar had never been before but had heard his Mum talk about the masses of trees and greenery and had been desperate to see it for himself. It was further than he thought, but the sight that awaited him was worth it. Bluebell Woods was beautiful. A mass of colour, with so many different kinds of trees of every shape and size.

"Do you know where we need to go now Bea?"

"The hive is towards the middle of the wood, by the stream. It's high in the old oak tree."

A little while later they reached a large tree and three metres above the ground was a strange looking object nestled amongst the branches. It hummed and moved and appeared to have a life all of its own.

"This is my home," said Bea proudly. "I should be able to make it from here. Thank you so much for helping me Oscar, you're a real friend." Bea climbed off Oscar's back and started to climb towards the hive.

"Can I come and visit you again Bea?"

"Anytime Oscar, you're always welcome."

He waited until Bea was safely in the hive, gave her a wave and set off for home.

That night he dreamed about flying and honey and big purple flowers. He loved being a cat, but being a bee was also quite exciting and he looked forward to seeing his new friend again.

A few days later Oscar was stood at the foot of the oak tree looking for Bea.

He craned his neck to see the hive and wondered of the best way to get her attention. He thought about climbing up, but it was very steep and he wasn't sure he'd be able to get down again.

His mum had told him how she had once got stuck in the tree at the bottom of the garden and Mr Martin had had to use a ladder to rescue her. Very embarrassing. No, Oscar would find another way.

"Bea, are you there Bea?" Oscar was shouting with all his might. "Bea, can you hear me?"

"What's all the racket about? Who are you and what do you want?" A large, elderly bumblebee had flown down from the hive and was obviously not very happy about all the noise.

"I'm sorry," said Oscar, "I didn't mean to disturb you. I'm looking for my friend Bea."

"Ah, you must be the young cat that Beatrice was talking about. I'm her Father, Mr Bumble."

"How is she? Is her wing better?" Oscar really wanted to see his friend.

"She's much better, but busy in the hive. I'll let her know you called."

"OK, thanks." Oscar tried to hide his disappointment as he turned round to head back through the woods. He dragged his paws as he wandered among the bluebells that towered over him.

One of the flowers just ahead was bobbing up and down, although there was no wind. Curious, Oscar crept low to the ground and stalked the flower.

"Buzzzzzzzz"

Oscar jumped, startled. Waving on top of the flower, trying to get his attention, was Bea.

"Hi Oscar. Dad said you called. I've finished my chores so he said I could come out to play. There's a lovely field not far from here with the most gorgeous flowers."

Bea buzzed ahead and Oscar ran behind. The field was beautiful, full of wild poppies that stood tall as soldiers, their red heads nodding slightly as Oscar passed by. The sky was bright blue and the sun shone like a precious gem. Oscar chased Bea and Bea chased Oscar. They were having so much fun together that they didn't notice a shadow being cast on the ground.

High above them, a kestrel was circling. He had spotted the little black and white creature running around in the field and was choosing his moment to swoop. Oscar was utterly unaware he was being watched by a beady eye and without warning, on silent wings, the bird nosedived towards the earth.

One minute Oscar was twisting and twirling in the poppies, the next he felt razor sharp talons sinking into his back. He yelped with pain as he was carried high into the air. Oscar struggled, but the kestrel's grip was too tight, and the more he moved the more it hurt.

"Bea, help me!" Oscar shouted out, but his cries were muffled by the whipping wind and the ground disappeared beneath him.

Bea was in shock, but knew she had to act and fast. Her wing still sore, she mustered up all her strength and flew back to the hive at a speed she'd never have thought possible.

"Dad come quick."

Mr Bumble poked his head out of the hive, "Beatrice, what is going on?"

"Dad it's an emergency. Oscar's been taken by a huge bird in the poppy field, he's in terrible danger! We have to help him!" Bea was close to tears.

Mr Bumble disappeared back into the hive and a moment later, the entire beehive population had gathered. He took immediate control and with great authority quickly explained what they needed to do.

"We must get the bird to circle lower. If he drops the cat from too high, he won't survive. Group one, locate the bird and distract him. Group two, use your flying tactics to force the bird down. Group three, soften the ground for landing. Remember, if the bird carries the cat to its nest, it's all over. All clear? Let's go!"

The swarm flew off at lightning speed as Bea watched helplessly. Her wing too damaged after the flight home to join them, she could only hope that the hive could save Oscar in time.

High in the sky, Oscar could feel the kestrel tiring. He was obviously heavier than the bird had first thought and there was once or twice Oscar thought he might drop him. He had tried talking to the bird, but it made no sound and didn't acknowledge his presence at all. Oscar was very scared and closed his eyes tight shut, trying to picture his mum and sisters and his warm, safe bed.

He had no idea how long they had been flying, but he could hear a strange humming noise. It got louder and louder and when he opened his eyes, the bird was surrounded by a swarm of bees.

"Keep calm," a deep, steady voice buzzed in Oscar's ear. "We're here to help you, but you must do exactly as we say." Oscar knew he must obey, his life depended on it.

The bee positioned himself close to Oscar's ear, where only he could hear. The kestrel was annoyed by the swarm, but was not losing height or changing direction.

"Jump when I say. Trust me. We'll get the bird to fly lower, but you must do it at once. Understand?"

Oscar nodded his head very slightly, scared the kestrel would hear him if he spoke.

The bees in the swarm then changed formation. Group one covered the bird's eyes. His sight lost, he stopped flying and hovered, motionless in the air, but still too high. Group two landed heavily on the bird's wings, weighing it down, forcing it to lose height. Below, group three marked out a landing area. A field with hay bales spread out. All they had to do was get the kestrel to release his grip at the right time.

The bee stayed in place near Oscar's ear and gave commands in a series of hums and buzzes that he didn't understand. Two bees flew down to the bird's claws, taking position by each foot. At the command, they struck their stings into the fleshy area above the claws. The kestrel let out a cry in shock, the pain made it open its talons and lose grip on its prey. Oscar was falling.

The bee buzzed instructions. "Now, prepare to land. Feet ready, nearly there. Three, two, one...landing."

Thud! Oscar came down to earth with some speed, but the bails softened his fall and he landed on his feet. He stayed low in the hay, afraid the bird would swoop down after him.

"Is it safe to come out yet?" Oscar was trembling, his eyes wide as he scanned the sky.

"You are safe now, but stay in the safety of the trees if you come to the woods again."

Oscar nodded, he could see the wood was only metres away, but it felt like miles.

When they got back to the hive, Bea was waiting. Her wing bent and her eyes puffy from crying. When she saw Oscar she ran up to him and gave him a huge hug.

Oscar turned to face the humming swarm of bees, "Thank you to each and every one of you for coming to my rescue today."

The swarm buzzed their appreciation and flew back into the hive to continue with their daily honey making.

A week later, Oscar was sunbathing in the garden when Sophie let out a scream. She jumped up and started running round the garden like a maniac.

"Sophie, what is it? Calm down!" Oscar got up and ran over to his sister. She was stood totally still, rigid with fear, pointing at the flower bed. A massive swarm of bees had gathered and were waving at Oscar. At the front was Bea, her wing mended and a big smile on her face.

"Hi Oscar. Hope you don't mind but I brought a few friends over to play."

Oscar and Bea raced round the garden laughing and playing.

"Hey, what's this?" Bea had landed on Oscar's head. A strange grey hair poked out from his shiny black fur, a grey hair that wouldn't lie flat.

"Uh oh – don't tell my Mum whatever you do. Our adventure with the kestrel has left its mark."

Oscar had used up another of his lives, as nine became six.

In his next adventure, instincts are what Oscar needs, to carry out this latest deed.

chapter 4

Blind faith

The Martins were expecting a visitor and the whole house was upside down.

Sally was running around the spare bedroom in a tizzy as Susie and Sophie moved food dishes and bedding around.

"What's going on?" said Oscar, quite confused by all the commotion. "Why is my bed by the window? Where's my favourite bowl?"

Sophie stopped what she was doing and looked at Oscar as though he was quite stupid.

"Really Oscar, you have the memory of a goldfish! Aunt Phoebe is arriving today and she'll need everything in a certain place."

"Why?" Oscar didn't remember everyone making such a fuss when Max paid a visit or when the Martins looked after next door's rabbit.

"Aunt Phoebe is blind!" replied Sally exasperated by Oscar's constant questions. "She can't see and will need everything arranged the way she's used to at her home. So the food is now next to the door and beds are by the window."

"Oh right, OK." Oscar felt bad for forgetting that Aunt Phoebe had special needs. He'd never met her before, but had heard she was very old and was going to be staying for a while, whilst her own family went on holiday.

"Well done girls, this looks lovely." Sally scanned the room one last time to double check everything was in place. "Oscar you can wait up and escort Aunt Phoebe to our room when she arrives."

"Typical," said Oscar to himself. "I get to show the old lady round, how totally boring!"

Ten minutes later a car pulled up outside the Martin house and a tall man with glasses and a slim lady with long blonde hair knocked on the front door. Mrs Martin welcomed her visitors and made everyone a cup of tea. The blonde lady was carrying a travel basket and placed it on the floor. Oscar crept into the living room to have a closer look and jumped back in surprise. Two luminous green orbs were staring back at him.

"Ah, here's our young Oscar," said Mrs Martin giving him a friendly squeeze. "I'm guessing he's wondering who's in the basket!"

"Aw, isn't he adorable," the blonde lady said as she picked Oscar up and put him on her knee. She smelt nice and tickled him under the chin. Oscar purred and wished this lady would stay rather than the old cat in the basket.

"He's a scamp all right, always up to mischief. I hope Phoebe copes with having kittens around, they can be quite a handful." Mrs Martin patted Oscar on the head and went in to the kitchen to make more tea.

The tall man with glasses walked over to the travel basket on the floor, "Let's see if the old girl copes," he said with a chuckle and flicked open the latch.

A few seconds later a beautiful tortoiseshell cat emerged, her fur a kaleidoscope of colour and the greenest eyes Oscar had ever seen. Aunt Phoebe stretched, yawned and leapt straight onto the blonde lady's knee. Oscar only just had time to move and landed with a thud on the floor.

"Oh dear, poor kitty, Phoebe didn't realise you were there, did you sweetheart?" The lady gave the multi-coloured cat a stroke.

Phoebe turned in Oscar's direction, her whiskers twitching and her big green eyes like round marbles.

"Sorry about that Oscar, are you OK?" her voice was smooth like silk. "I've heard so much about you! How many grey hairs now?"

Oscar was surprised that Aunt Phoebe knew about his grey hairs. In fact Aunt Phoebe was full of surprises, as Oscar would soon find out. She didn't look or sound old at all and certainly didn't act or talk like she was blind. Curiosity got the better of him and he simply had to ask.

"Aunt Phoebe, what's it like, being blind?"

"Not as bad as you think. My other senses work better now, I can smell a sardine a mile away," she said with a smile.

Oscar was amazed at how confident she was. She jumped off the blonde lady's knee, rubbed against the tall man's legs and then walked straight out of the room and headed for the stairs!

"Aunt Phoebe, wait up!" Oscar ran after her, "Mum said I had to escort you to the room. Do you need to hold onto my tail or something?"

Aunt Phoebe laughed, "Of course not, I'll be fine, you lead the way and I'll follow."

When they reached the steep spiral staircase that led to the attic room Oscar stopped and wondered how Aunt Phoebe would cope.

"Is everything alright Oscar?"

"Yes, it's just the next bit is a little tricky even for me and I can see!"

"Describe it to me in as much detail as you can."

Oscar concentrated really hard. He explained there were twelve steps, the third one had a bit missing near the edge and the eighth one was a bit wobbly.

"Perfect. You've painted a picture in my head and I'll now save that in my memory. Here we go..." Aunt Phoebe then sprinted up the stairs faster than Oscar ever dared, leaving him opened mouthed, totally in awe of his Aunt.

"Wow! That was amazing, even Mum isn't that quick!"

"We are all capable of a lot more than we give ourselves credit for," Aunt Phoebe said as she walked confidently into the attic room.

Oscar loved having Aunt Phoebe over, she was good fun and had some amazing stories to tell. Before she came to live with the blonde lady, she had lived on a farm with a lot of other cats. Their job had been to keep the rats and mice away from the barn and farm house. One night she had been out hunting when she was attacked by a fox. Aunt Phoebe had fought back, swiping with her claws, hissing and spitting. The fox ran off, but Aunt Phoebe was in a sorry state by the time she'd crawled back to the farm house. When the farmer found her she was unconscious and then spent a week in intensive care. The vet had saved her life, but her sight was affected by her injuries and within a few weeks she was blind.

She could no longer work on the farm, so the blonde lady took her in. Aunt Phoebe had missed the other cats at first, but soon got used to her new life. The kittens all loved to hear Aunt Phoebe's stories and every night before bed, she would tell them a story of life on the farm. The time the lambs were born in the field, riding on the back of a pony called Old Norris and chasing a dog that was bothering the chickens.

Oscar was also learning to listen more closely to what Aunt Phoebe called 'instincts', she explained it as a feeling, a knowing, that all animals have and should listen to. Oscar's instincts were definitely improving. He could sense things more easily and his whiskers twitched more when his eyes were closed, like his very own personal radar.

It was coming to the end of Aunt Phoebe's stay and Oscar was very sad to say goodbye. He'd really enjoyed learning new things, he was now able to walk the length of the fence with his eyes shut and had knocked seconds off his fastest time up the spiral staircase. On Aunt Phoebe's last day, Oscar wanted to do something special for her. She had mentioned that when she was on the farm she loved a wild flower called catnip. Oscar wanted to collect some of the flowers to give as a present to Aunt Phoebe before she went home.

He left the house and headed for Arlington Meadows. As Oscar got closer to the meadow he could see that something wasn't quite right. There was a large metal fence around the boundary of the field and a big sign said, "Construction site – no unauthorized entry." The meadow was full of big yellow digging machines and a lot of the flowers had been trampled and squashed.

As he approached the gate, there was a rumbling noise behind him and in the distance he saw a delivery truck making its way towards the gate. He quickly hid in the bushes and waited for the truck to get closer. When a man got out of the truck to unlock the gate, Oscar saw his chance and dashed though the opening.

Once inside Oscar was amazed at the change in the meadow. There was very little greenery left and most of the ground was muddy with deep track marks. As the man unloaded the lorry, Oscar explored the site in search of the catnip.

He had almost given up when he suddenly spotted a plant poking out from behind a large cement bucket. It was white with purple spots and as he got closer the smell was fantastic. He reached the plant and took a big sniff and suddenly he wanted to leap around and be silly. Aunt Phoebe had said the plant was popular with the farm cats and now he knew why, he was floating on a cloud, then flying in the sky. Oscar was so busy rolling around and enjoying himself, that he didn't notice the man and the lorry had gone. He was locked inside the site with no way of getting out.

An hour passed and Oscar started to get worried. He had promised he'd be home for tea and in time to say goodbye to Aunt Phoebe. Judging from how the sun was starting to set, it wouldn't be long before the night crept in. He was desperate to get home and had walked the perimeter of the fence a hundred times and there was no way out. The metal mesh and barbed wire made it impossible to climb. He was feeling very glum and a little bit scared. The machines were casting big, dark shadows on the ground and he kept hearing strange noises. He'd tried meowing as loudly as he could, but there was no-one to hear him so it seemed pointless. He thought about Aunt Phoebe and what she would do in such a situation. She would take note of her 'instincts'. Oscar decided to do just that.

He sat on an upturned cement bucket and quietened his mind. He closed his eyes and listened. At first there was nothing; no sounds, no pictures, nothing. Then gradually he started to sense something. There was a faint scratching sound coming from somewhere nearby. He concentrated, trying to pinpoint exactly where it was coming from. He opened his eyes and his vision settled on a large plank of wood. He went over to have a closer look and realised it was covering a hole in the ground.

He pushed the plank a little and peered down the hole. It was completely dark and a bit smelly. The scratching noise was getting closer. He moved to hide behind the bucket, just in time to see a big brown rat come out of the hole and scurry away. Oscar was certain the hole must lead somewhere because as he sat there, another rat disappeared into the darkness beneath the ground. Gingerly, he lowered himself down, his claws acting at miniature anchors. It was damp, dark and the stench clung to his nostrils. It was getting steeper and he could feel his paws slipping in the slime as the darkness wrapped around him.

He kept thinking of Aunt Phoebe and how she had taught him to rely on his senses. He concentrated and used his whiskers to feel his way, pricking his ears up for any sounds that might help him find a way out. Oscar had been crawling in the tunnel for some time, the occasional rat had scurried past, but not stopped to talk.

Then he heard a noise that seemed familiar. It was a rushing sound and the air was getting cooler and fresher. The tunnel had reached the outside and had opened up by the stream at the bottom of the woods.

Oscar had a real dislike of water after his first mishap with the washing machine. This water was even worse. Freezing cold, disgustingly dirty and he had no idea how deep it was. He looked around for something to jump onto or climb, but there was nothing close by. There was no way around it, he would have to jump in. He took a deep breath and *splash*, in he went!

The cold whipped around his body and his wet fur was dragging him under. He tried to get a foot hold, but the part he was in was too deep. His only option was to try and stay afloat long enough to be swept downstream and into the shallows. He tried to grab an overhanging willow branch by the waters, but missed and went under the water. Spluttering for breath, his eyes stinging, he knew he mustn't panic. He thought about Aunt Phoebe and her advice to use his instincts. He focused and became quite still, and, as he stopped fighting the water, he found he floated better. The freezing murkiness was clinging to his body, but he wasn't going to be beaten by it. He spotted a branch and this time he was ready. He lunged, grabbed and pulled himself to the muddy bank. Bedraggled and cold, he dragged himself up the side of the bank.

It was nearly eight o'clock when Oscar finally arrived home, looking a very sorry state.

"Oscar! Where have you been? we've all been worried sick!" Mrs Martin scooped him up and wrapped him in a towel.

"Oh Oscar you're covered in mud and smell awful!" Bella was right. Mr Martin quickly ran some warm water in the kitchen sink and plonked him in it. He was so tired he couldn't be bothered to fight, and knew he'd feel better once he was clean and dry again.

"Oscar, I'm going now," Aunt Phoebe was gently stroking his head. "It looks like you have another reminder of your adventure tonight." She tried to smooth down the wiry grey tell-tale hair that refused to lie flat.

Oscar had used up another of his lives, as nine became five.

In his next adventure, Oscar has a spooky meeting when he goes out trick or treating.

chapter 5

Spooked!

It was Halloween and Bella was busy carving a pumpkin lantern while Mrs Martin finished making her a witch outfit with a pointy hat and wand. The black velvet dress was covered in cobwebs made from bits of old lace and had a pretend spider that dangled from the sleeve. Bella twirled around in her new dress and hat.

"Hi Oscar, do I look scary?" Bella pulled a witchy face and Oscar rubbed his head against her ankle to show he approved of her spooky outfit.

Bella and Oscar were soon outside, closely followed by Mrs Martin holding the pumpkin lantern. After Bella had knocked on all the doors of Arlingon Grove and had a pocketful of sweets, it was time to go home for a supper of pumpkin soup.

Oscar was quite happy in the cool October night and wanted to see if he could find any more witches or wizards to help. He saw a few children with lanterns, but no-one seemed interested in having a cat tag along. He stopped to climb a big old oak to see if he could spot any more trick or treaters. The tree was starting to lose its leaves, but Oscar could hear a rustling. Wondering what was making the noise, he climbed a bit higher. The noise was definitely coming from above and when Oscar climbed a bit higher, he nearly fell off with surprise. A massive bird with big round eyes was looking right at him.

"Can I ask what you are doing in my tree?" asked the owl with a frosty tone and a steely stare.

"Oh I'm sorry, I didn't mean to…I was just…" Oscar was a bit scared of this big, round-eyed bird.

"Typical, no respect for elders and totally ill-equipped to answer the simplest of questions."

The owl then swivelled his head round to face the opposite direction.

"Whoa! How did you do that? Does it go all the way round?"

"You really are a curious little creature! Of course it doesn't go all the way round, it would drop off! Now what do you want?" The owl turned his head back again and ruffled his feathers for effect.

"I was looking to see if there were any more children I could help for Halloween."

"I see. Well I think it's a little late for children to be out now, but I know somewhere that is always ....interesting on All Hallows Eve," the owl said mysteriously.

"Where's that? Could you show me?" Oscar was quite enthralled by this strange bird that seemed to know so much.

"I'll point you in the right direction, but I'm not flying yet. It's still too early for me, the moon is barely visible."

Oscar looked towards the night sky and could see that the moon was full, but also shrouded by clouds.

The owl pointed his wing towards the north and hushed his voice. In a whisper he said, "Only the bravest may enter, those of a nervous nature should turn back. The house on the hill is ever so still, at least on first glance. Then you notice something is a little...strange!"

Oscar was mesmerised by the bird's words and wanted to explore the house on the hill straight away.

It took him almost half an hour to get to the house but as the clouds parted, the light of the moon showed the way. When Oscar arrived at the bottom of the hill, he had to crawl under an old wrought iron gate to get into the walled grounds. Even from a distance, he could see the house was mostly boarded up, graffiti scrawled across it. The other windows were broken and the garden was completely overgrown with brambles. Oscar was careful not to catch himself on any of the sharp thorns, but it was tricky as the path was so littered with weeds. He saw a crack of light coming from a downstairs window and worked his way up to the sill to have a better look. Inside the house was as decrepit as the outside. Cobwebs and dust covered the broken bits of old furniture. A small table held a single candle, its tiny flame casting eerie shadows around the room.

He crept through the broken window, excited to explore. Downstairs was dark and gloomy, the broken floor tiles in the hall were cold under his paws and Oscar wished he could wear woolly socks like Bella. The kitchen was totally bare except for an old-style sink in the corner with a tap that dripped every few seconds. The *drip drop* noise sounded quite loud in the silence of the old house.

Oscar moved into what should have been the lounge with the small table and candle. There was a dusty armchair, a bundle of old newspapers and a fireplace that hadn't seen a blazing fire for a long time. Oscar couldn't figure out how the candle had been lit, surely no-one lived in this dirty, dishevelled old house?

He walked past the table and the flame of the candle cast a shadow of him across the wall as he moved. He crossed the room and headed for the stairs, a huge sweeping staircase that must have been magnificent once, but the spindles were broken and the handrail was chipped and cracked. The stairs creaked as he climbed up them to the landing.

Once at the top, Oscar was faced with four doors, all shut and heavy looking. One by one, he tried nudging them with his nose, but none of the doors would open.

"Excuse me, can I help you?"

Oscar jumped a metre in the air! Out of nowhere a sleek black cat was standing next to him.

"Hello! Sorry you scared me. I was just seeing if any of the doors would open." Oscar looked sheepish and hung his head, knowing he was no doubt in trouble for tres-pawing.

"All the doors are locked and only I have the key," the black cat then turned and started walking down the hall away from Oscar.

"Hey, wait!" Oscar followed the cat, "Do you live here? What's your name?"

The cat stopped and turned to face Oscar.

"My name is Ebony and yes I live here, but what might I ask are you doing in my house?"

There was something about this cat that didn't seem quite right, but he couldn't quite put his paw on it. He could feel the black cat's eyes boring right into him.

"I came here to explore, I met an owl who said the house was....interesting, but I promise I didn't know anyone lived here." Oscar trailed off, not sure if he was making any sense.

Ebony looked at Oscar and shook her head "Mr Woo really should know better, I've told him before to stop interfering."

"You know him?"

"Oh yes, I've known him since he was a chick, and his father before him and his father before him."

Oscar was puzzled, he thought Mr Woo was quite old yet Ebony seemed fairly young.

As if she had read his mind, Ebony said, "Appearances are deceiving, not everything is always as it seems."

She then walked towards the first door that Oscar had tried to open and without even touching it, it swung open.

"Whoa! How did you do that?" Oscar asked in amazement.

"To you this was a locked door, to me it was simply a door that wanted to be asked first."

"What do you mean? You spoke to the door?" Oscar was very confused now.

"Exactly. In my head I politely asked if it would be so kind as to open, and it did. It's very simple. Good manners are always important, you ask the door opposite if it would care to open."

Ebony was talking as if it was the most normal thing in the

world and Oscar really wasn't sure what to do. Not wanting to offend her, he concentrated really hard and in his head asked the door to open.

The door stayed firmly shut and Oscar felt a bit silly.

"Did you say the magic word?" Ebony was looking intently at Oscar and then at the door.

"What? Please?" Oscar thought for a second. Did he say please? He wasn't sure. He tried it again, this time he made sure that he was very polite and said 'please.'

The door swung open and Oscar nearly fell down the stairs in surprise.

"Excellent work," beamed Ebony.

The room was beautiful, with a high ceiling and a beautiful crystal chandelier hanging from the centre. The walls were a soft pink and in the middle of the room was an old fashioned bedstead carved from wood and painted the same pastel shade. Toys and teddy bears lined the walls, china dolls with painted faces exquisitely dressed in Victorian style clothes, a colourful Jack-in-the-Box in the corner and a rocking horse with a silky mane and tail.

"Wow," said Oscar. "Whose room is this?"

"It's Lottie's room. She is my ….my….." Ebony trailed off, unable to find the right words.

"Is she your human friend like Bella is to me? Bella's great, we have so much fun together."

Ebony looked wistful, then smiled and continued.

"Yes, she was my special human. I used to lay by the hearth and she'd stroke me and sing nursery rhymes."

"Where is she now?" Oscar asked puzzled.

"It was a long time ago when Lottie lived here. It's just me now." Ebony seemed sad and Oscar wanted to ask more questions, but had a feeling that she wasn't ready to say any more.

Oscar left Ebony in Lottie's room and asked the door opposite to open, remembering to say 'please'. It swung open and Oscar was in another bedroom. The bed was the biggest he had ever seen, with a large post at either corner and heavy velvet material draped over them. The bedding was faded green silk embroidered with lace. Oscar couldn't resist jumping on it to see if it was as comfortable as it looked. He leapt up and snuggled into the eiderdown, the soft goose feathers wrapping around him and he started to yawn. He closed his eyes and drifted off to sleep.

Oscar woke up with a start. Something felt different, but he was groggy and couldn't figure out what had changed. A noise from downstairs made him sit bolt upright and he strained his ears to listen. He could hear a strange cracking sound and he jumped off the bed to investigate. As he opened the door to the landing, a sudden surge of heat and smoke engulfed him. The house was on fire!

Trying not to panic, his first thought was to find Ebony. He quickly ran to Lottie's room, but she was nowhere to be seen.

"Ebony!" Oscar shouted as best he could, "Where are you?"

The timber frame of the house was burning like kindling and the flames were starting to lick up the staircase. Thick black smoke was swirling everywhere. Oscar crawled on his belly, struggling to breathe and desperate to find his friend and a way out. The heat was singeing his fur and he was very scared. Moments later the floor started to crack and before he knew what was happening he was falling.

"Oscar? Oscar? Can you hear me? Oscar please wake up, please Oscar."

His head felt like a lead weight and his body ached. He slowly opened his eyes.

Oscar realised he was outside, away from the house on a patch of grass. He looked towards the house and saw the fire brigade tackling the flames.

"What happened Ebony? The last thing I remember was falling through the floor towards the fire!"

"You had a lucky escape. You landed on the old couch; I found you and dragged you outside."

Oscar was lost for words. Ebony had risked her own life to save his.

Ebony said the candle downstairs had fallen over, catching the pile of old newspapers. It hadn't taken long for the blaze to get going and engulf the downstairs. Ebony had heard the floor break and seen him fall, then managed to drag him to safety.

Oscar was totally speechless. He'd had some scrapes in his time, but Ebony's bravery and quick thinking was something else.

"How can I ever thank you Ebony? I owe you my life."

Oscar was worried and wondered where she would live now her house was nothing more than a charred shell.

"Don't you worry about me, I'll be just fine. I really think we should get you home now, your family will be very worried."

Oscar's heart sank. His mum would be furious that he'd been out so long and got into trouble again.

Ebony knew some short cuts back to Oscar's house, although she kept saying how different everything looked. They reached the back door of the Martin's house and Sally was sat waiting on the doorstep with a very stern look on her face.

"Where on earth have you been Oscar? I've had half the cats in the neighbourhood looking for you."

"Sorry mum, so much has happened," and he started to retell his adventure.

"And you say your new friend, Ebony, pulled you from a burning building and walked you home?" Sally didn't look impressed at all.

"Yes Mum, she's over there by the tree." Oscar waved at Ebony, who raised a paw back.

"Well either my eyesight isn't what it used to be or you're telling a very tall story. There is no black cat by the tree!"

Oscar started to argue, but then looked towards the tree and Ebony was gone.

"She was there a second ago!" Oscar said indignantly.

In the morning Oscar went to the old oak tree to find Mr Woo and tell him about what had happened.

"Ah, I see you survived the trip to the house on the hill," said Mr Woo.

"Only just!" said Oscar excitedly. "A fire started and I fell through the floor and Ebony saved me."

"A fire! My goodness how terrible. What a dreadful palaver!"

Mr Woo was clearly upset.

"As usual I am left to explain the complicated bits, this is going to come as a bit of a shock."

Oscar was totally unprepared for what Mr Woo told him. He explained that Ebony wasn't an earth cat anymore, but a spirit cat. She had lived in the house over a hundred years ago with her family and their daughter Lottie. One Halloween, when Lottie was only five years old, she'd fallen from the nursery window. Ebony never got over losing the little girl and blamed herself for not being able to prevent the accident. Even when she herself passed away many years later, her spirit felt bound to the house. Mr Woo said that because Ebony had saved Oscar's life and the house was now gone, it had released her and she could be reunited with Lottie and her family again.

Oscar sat totally still, utterly mesmerised by what Mr Woo was saying. He'd known there was something different about Ebony, but had never once thought she was a ghost!

As Oscar walked home, he thought about all the strange twists and turns of his latest adventure. He would always remember Ebony, the wiry grey hair that stuck up from his fur made sure of that, as nine lives became four.

In his next adventure, a four legged friend's in need and Oscar performs an heroic deed.

Chapter 6

A dog's life

It was December and the Martins were going to spend Christmas visiting family in London. Oscar and his sisters had been booked into the Pet's Plaza, a hotel built especially for cats and dogs. Oscar was not happy at the thought of being cooped up with his sisters for a week.

When they arrived at Pet's Plaza, Oscar was pleasantly surprised. Their enclosure was clean and bright, with an indoor heated area where the beds were and an undercover outdoor section for playing. Rachel, the lady owner, made a real fuss of all the cats, giving them tuna treats and stroking their fur.

Oscar sat on the tree stump observing his surroundings. He could see the main building, it looked like an old stone-built farmhouse, the chimney poking out from the roof at a lopsided angle and smoke swirling out into the sky. As he watched the clouds pass by he wondered if Bella had gotten to London yet or if she could see the same clouds he was looking at.

A few days later, early one morning, Oscar was woken by a sound. Half asleep, he went into the outside enclosure to see what was going on. In the half darkness he could make out a shape heading at speed towards the cat's area. As it got closer, and Oscar could focus, he saw a brown, scruffy dog running full pelt and heading straight for the enclosure. He skidded to a halt, right outside Oscar's pen. The dog was very thin and bits of its fur were missing, Oscar wondered when it had last eaten and hoped moggy wasn't on the menu.

The dog, suddenly noticing Oscar, turned to face him and growled,

"Don't make a sound"

"Why?" Oscar was more curious than scared of this raggedy creature.

"Shhhh….they'll hear you."

Two men, one tall and thin and the other short and stout, were snooping around the field outside. One had a stick and a rope and the other a net; both were talking in hushed tones.

"I'm sure he came in here. If I get my hands on him, I'll wring his neck!" said the short one.

"He's mincemeat alright. We'll be the ones in hot water if we don't find him though," replied the thin one.

The men were heading towards the cat enclosure and Oscar didn't like the sound of them at all. Without a thought for his own safety, Oscar knew he had to do something to help. If the dog stayed where he was, he would get caught. He needed to hide him.

"Listen, can you reach the bolt on the gate into our pen? Slide it over and come in, quick before they find you!"
The dog turned towards the little cat and his eyes showed his surprise, but also his gratitude for the gesture of trust and kindness. He stood on his hind legs and gripped the bolt with his mouth. It slipped a few times, but then it moved and the gate swung open.

The dog crept into the caged area and lay down at the back, panting heavily. Oscar was worried the men would hear him. He quickly went inside, but the area was too small to fit the dog in too. Oscar grabbed his blanket from his bed and dragged it outside.

The dog was shivering with the cold and his eyes showed how scared he was of being found.

"You'll be safe here" said Oscar, trying to sound reassuring. He placed the blanket over the dog and then pushed his water bowl towards him.

"Thank you, I don't know what to say" the dog lapped up the water thirstily.

"I'm going to have a look outside to see if they are still around." Oscar slipped out of the gate quietly and reached the fence that separated the enclosure from the field. He couldn't see the men anywhere and was satisfied that they had given up.

The dog was hiding under the blanket, but sat up when Oscar said the men had gone. Oscar could count his ribs and see skin through his fur.

"Who were those horrible men?"

"They work for a man who runs a warehouse a few miles from here. I was a stray dog living on the streets. I found scraps to eat, streams to drink from. Life was tough but I survived. Then one day, I was prowling around the factory looking for something to eat. The tall man coaxed me in with a bacon sandwich and the next thing I know, I'm tied to a post. I'm supposed to guard the grounds, but they feed me so little I barely have enough energy to stand. If I try to escape they beat me with a stick." The dog hung his head sadly.

Oscar was horrified. He'd never come across any kind of cruelty before, the only humans he'd ever had contact with were loving ones. He couldn't imagine anyone intentionally hurting him and he felt very sorry for the dog.

"You can rest here until morning. I've got a bit of food left which you're welcome to have." Oscar pushed his bowl over and the dog ate the leftovers in seconds.

"Thank you. As soon as the sun rises, I'll make a move."

Oscar slept the rest of the night outside sharing his blanket with his new friend. He wondered if his sisters would believe his story in the morning.

Just as the morning light appeared and the natural world was starting to wake, two men, one tall and thin, one short and stout, opened the van door. In the lane by the field, as the sun rose, their hunt continued.

The thin man crept into the cat's enclosure and was peering inside pens. He brushed past a cage, waking the two Siamese cats.

"Meow meow," Yin said loudly.

"Mew mew," Yang replied.

"Shut up," the man growled. "Flaming cats, good for nothing!"

Oscar woke up, a little stiff from the cold, but hearing Yin and Yang had alerted his senses. He nudged the dog and whispered for him to stay still and quiet. He pulled the blanket over the dog and stood protectively in front of him.

"Now then, what have we here?" The thin man had a sharp pointed nose and was poking it into the cage. "I think the little kitty needs to shift itself, or it'll feel the force of my...." And he slammed a stick into the cage with such force, it bent the wire.

Oscar stood his ground and hissed at the man, puffing up his coat until his fur stood on end, claws sharp and ready. The rest of the cats had been woken by the commotion and were shocked to see the man waving a large stick at Oscar. The man was approaching fast and Oscar had to think quick.

At the top of his voice he shouted,

"I need you to make a much noise as possible to let Rachel know we have an intruder - one, two, three go!"
MEOW….MEOW….MEOW….MEOW

All the cats in all the pens burst into vocal harmony. The noise was phenomenal. The kitchen light went on in the farmhouse.

Not put off, the man burst into their cage and all Oscar could think about was protecting his new friend. He leapt at the man, his claws fully extended, landing skilfully on the arm carrying the stick. Sharp points sank into the flesh and the man screamed in pain. He dropped the weapon but was bleeding and now even angrier.

The dog was whimpering, scared and in shock, but Oscar knew this was his only chance to escape.

"Quick, run out now, while I distract him." Oscar was clawing the man's leg as he hopped about, trying to shake him off. Oscar lost his grip and flew through the air. As he fell, the man brought his boot up and kicked Oscar in the side.

Oscar yowled in agony, his ribcage felt as though it had exploded. "That'll teach you!" the man snarled and whacked him again. Oscar heard a crack and felt dizzy with pain.

The dog raced past the tall man, but didn't see the other man with a net. He was backed into a corner. At that exact moment Rachel appeared in her dressing gown and wellies to see what all the noise was about.

"What on earth is going on? Who are you and what are you doing on my land?" Rachel was flustered and visibly shaking at finding intruders in the cat enclosure with a net over a dog.

"Sorry to bother you Miss," said the tall man. "This dog was trying to attack the cats. We got here just in time. No worries, we'll sort it out."

Oscar couldn't believe the lies he was hearing! Despite the terrible pain in his ribs, he dragged himself over to the dog cowering in the net. He stood boldly in front of him, hissing at the men if they came near. Rachel noticed that the tall man had scratches on his arm and saw the wooden stick in the enclosure. She was worried. Oscar looked hurt and she knew he wasn't a vicious cat and would only have attacked if provoked. She knew something wasn't right.

"Leave the dog here, I have a spare kennel. I'll deal with him and try and find his owner." Rachel went over to the dog and was shocked to see how malnourished and weak he was.

"No need for that, he's a stray. We'll, erm, take him to the dog pound on our way to work," said the short man.

Rachel scooped Oscar up and watched in horror as the men bundled the dog into the back of the van. As they drove off, she got out her mobile and made a call.

The emergency vet arrived half an hour later to take a look at Oscar. He was trying to be brave, but the pain was excruciating. As the vet examined him, it was obvious that the kick had broken three of his ribs.

At the warehouse, the thin man was smoking a cigarette when two cars with flashing lights pulled into the yard. Three police officers got out and started to question him and the short man. Voices were raised and they were both bundled into the back of one of the cars in handcuffs.

A policewoman went over to see the dog. He wagged his tail and she carefully untied the chain and led him into the other car where a blanket was laid on the back seat.

As the vet's car was going, another car pulled up. A policewoman got out and asked Rachel some questions.

Oscar had been resting in front of the fire, but opened his eyes when he heard the lounge door open. Next to Rachel was his new friend the dog, who, only hours earlier, he thought was gone forever.

"He's had a rocky start in life, Oscar, but he's a real fighter, so I've called him Rocky," said Rachel.

Rocky walked over to Oscar, licked his face and sat down next to him on the rug where the two friends curled up and went to sleep.

Three days later, the Martins came to collect the cats and Rachel told them all about Oscar's latest adventure and the stray dog. Bella was hugging Oscar as he nuzzled against her face, then Rocky licked Bella's nose and she hugged him too. The three of them looked so happy that Mr Martin said, "Rachel, I know just the family to give a stray dog a home." Rocky settled into family life perfectly and Oscar was so thrilled to have his new best friend in the house. It was even worth having another wiry grey hair that wouldn't lie straight, as nine lives became three!

In his next adventure, he wants to be the best in show, but to what lengths will he have to go?

Chapter 7

Best in show

Oscar was watching Bella's ballet class from outside on the window ledge. He loved to see her twisting and turning in time to the music. This Saturday, Bella left class clutching a leaflet. It was advertising Pet Factor at the Village Hall and Bella wanted to enter all her pets in the competition.

The run up to the show was a new experience for Oscar. Bella had decided to enter him into the "Catrabatics" category and was training him to do movements in time to the music. She had choreographed a routine and Oscar found it easy.

Rocky was being entered into the "Most Obedient" category as Bella had been teaching him to "sit", "stay" and "roll over" on demand. Rocky was a natural and he quickly learnt to do exactly what she said. Bella also entered Sophie into the "Prettiest Kitty" and Susie into the "Purriest Puss" categories.

The night before the show, Bella spent an hour brushing and grooming Oscar, his sisters and Rocky until their coats gleamed.

"Hey Oscar," Rocky was lying by the fire, "Do you think we stand much chance of winning tomorrow?"

Oscar walked over and curled up next to his friend, "As good a chance as anyone else."

"I'm feeling quite nervous." Rocky sat up and stared into the fire, "I've never done anything like this before. I'm just a stray dog that got lucky."

Oscar couldn't believe Rocky would think that, "Don't be silly, there's no better dog in this whole town, you'll be great! Even if we don't win, it doesn't matter, Bella will still love us."

Rocky looked a bit happier, but Oscar could tell he was still worried.

Saturday morning at the Village Hall was a hive of activity. Bella signed a form to enter and they took their place next to a man with a very old cat called Charlie. Oscar wondered how old he was, his black fur was turning brown and his eyes were a little cloudy, but he seemed quite alert.

"Hi," he said to Charlie. "What are you entering today?"

Charlie took a creaky step forward. "I thought that might have been obvious lad," he chuckled. "I'm in the agility class!"

He stretched out his back leg to demonstrate he was still supple.

Oscar's face must have looked shocked because Charlie laughed and added, "Only kidding! I've been entered into the "Senior" category. Basically, the oldest cat wins and at nineteen, I'm guaranteed to win! What category are you?"

"I'm in the "Catrabatics" show," said Oscar proudly.

"Very good lad. I won that ten years ago, still have the rosette at home. The one you really want to win is "Best in Show". There's a good prize if you get that one, but the competition is fierce this year."

He nodded his head towards a table by the window. A cat the colour of pure snow with huge blue-grey eyes was sat washing herself. Her face was flat and her fur much longer than any other cat Oscar had met.

"Who's that?" he whispered to Charlie.

"That's Snowdrop the Third," he said. "Three generations of her family have won the title and this year, she is determined to get it. She's a pedigree Persian and has real catittude!"

Oscar looked at Snowdrop and her perfectly white fur and unusual features.

Snowdrop caught him staring at her and instantly stopped grooming.

"What are you looking at? Has nobody told you it's rude to stare!" Snowdrop's voice was cool and she pronounced her words with great precision.

"Oh, I'm sorry. I was just admiring your coat."

Snowdrop sat upright and admired her gleaming fur.

"Yes, I am very beautiful. I come from a pedigree line with true star quality, unlike some others here." She cast a snooty glance in Charlie's direction.

"Come on Oscar, I'll show you around. I may not look great, but no-one knows this show better than me!" Charlie nudged Oscar and they left Snowdrop to her preening.

Charlie led the way through the throngs of people who had come to the pet show and made his way to the main field. There was a dalmatian in high spirits pulling on her lead. She could smell the sausages on the barbeque and was desperate to try one.

"Hi Sheba, need a helping paw?"

Charlie had jumped onto a nearby chair and was now eye level with the excited dog.

Sheba grinned at Charlie and the old cat leapt off the seat and headed for the barbeque. Oscar watched as he crept stealth-like towards the grill, waiting until the man cooking the food turned to greet someone. Quick as a flash he leapt up and grabbed a sausage. Seconds later he was back and he flicked the sausage in the air and Sheba gulped it down in one bite. Oscar was very impressed.

The old cat touched noses with the spotty dog and beckoned for Oscar to follow him.

They wandered back to the main tent and saw Rocky curled up underneath a table.

"I'd like you to meet my new friend Charlie," said Oscar.

Rocky looked up and attempted a smile for his best friend but it wasn't very convincing.

"Sorry Oscar, I'm feeling really nervous and I'm sure I'm going to make a mess of everything and let Bella down."

Charlie coughed and cleared his throat, "If you don't mind me saying, I think you're being rather hard on yourself. I watched you practise and you were very good. I've been to this show every year since I was a kitten and I can give you a few pointers. A lot of it is about looking and acting confident, even if you're feeling nervous or scared."

Rocky sat up and pricked his ears. Anything that helped him improve was worth listening to.

"Firstly, always walk close to your owner and stand tall. A droopy head or saggy tail will give the wrong impression. The judges want you to enjoy the experience so your body language is very important. Be quick to respond to your owner's commands with enthusiasm, but not too much. My friend Sheba always loses points by getting over excited in the ring. Lastly and most importantly, go into the ring knowing you can win. If you think like a winner, you will act like a winner!"

Rocky had already changed his position. He sat up straight with a determined gleam in his eye. The pep talk had worked like magic.

"Ladies and gentlemen, please take your places in the main hall," the tannoy announcer instructed. "We will be starting with the "Most Obedient Dog" category."

For a brief moment a look of panic swept across Rocky's face. Then he stood up tall, head held high, ready for Bella to walk him to the hall.

In the hall a dozen other dogs in all shapes and sizes had lined up as owners were given numbers to pin onto their clothes. The three "Pet Factor" judges were seated on the stage at a large wooden table covered with a plush velvet tablecloth. They looked very regal and important.

The first dog in the ring was a droopy-eared Spaniel called Percy. He was very obedient, but quite slow around the course. Ali the Boxer dog was next, but ran out of energy halfway round and sat down for a rest. His owner had to carry him off looking embarrassed.

Then it was Rocky's turn. Bella was very proud as she led him into the ring. He walked tight next to her legs, tail wagging and head held high. He performed the commands perfectly, sitting, lying down, offering a paw. Once all the dogs had performed, the judges went into a small room to confer and a few minutes later, emerged to announce the results.

Mr Macintosh the local vet and senior judge spoke into the microphone. "All dogs performed well, but we have arrived at a result. In third place Percy, a very sound and solid entrant. In second place Sheba, a restrained yet enthusiastic performance. In first place, an entrant who impressed us with his confidence, skill and speed. The winner for "Most Obedient Dog" is...Rocky."

The crowd started clapping and cheering and Oscar ran up to his friend glowing with pride. "Well done Rocky, I knew you could do it, you were amazing."

Rocky was grinning from ear to ear and Bella was jumping around in excitement.

The pressure was now on. Oscar really wanted to prove he too was a champion. The tannoy announcer informed them that the "Catrabatics" would be starting in five minutes. Bella picked up Oscar and headed for the arena.

Oscar felt exhilarated at the prospect of performing in front of an audience, but a little bit nervous as well. He remembered what Charlie has told Rocky about thinking like a winner and he waited his turn, telling himself over and over again that he could do it.

"Contestant number 4, Bella with Oscar."

Oscar sat statue like on the small table, not a whisker moved as he waited for the music to start. Bella gave Mr Martin a nod, he pressed play on the machine and right on cue, Oscar started his routine. He was leaping in the air, spinning, twisting and turning. The audience making "ooohs" and "ahhhhs" as he climbed up to the highest rung of a tall ladder and somersaulted off the top, landing on all four feet at the exact point the music stopped. The audience went wild, clapping and cheering. Oscar walked out of the ring feeling proud that he had done his best. Once all the cats had performed, the judges once again went into a little room to decide on the winner.

Mrs Davis, a local pet shop owner and judge, walked on stage and took the microphone.

"Ladies and gentleman, we have made a decision regarding the winner of the "Catrobatics" competition....."

BOOM!

There was a huge noise. A large wall caved in just behind the stage. The room was filled full of panic, a thick cloud of dust swirled in the air with rubble and debris littering the floor. The kitchen wall was completely gone. People were shouting, running for the exits, dogs were barking, cats meowing and in the confusion, nobody noticed a single cat carrier caught under a fallen piece of timber. Blue-grey eyes looked out terrified, the white fur covered in dust. Mrs Whiting-Smythe had left her prize possession and no-one was looking for Snowdrop the Third.

Everyone was very shaken by the sudden explosion, but miraculously no-one was seriously hurt. The fire brigade arrived and cordoned off the building, saying that they suspected a gas explosion and that it wasn't safe to go inside. The lady organiser had a register and was calling out names and ticking people off on the list. A head count confirmed that all the children and adults had managed to get out, but there was a commotion at the far end of the car park. Mrs Whiting-Smythe was screaming at a fireman, demanding that he go in and find her prize Persian. He was very calm and explained to the hysterical lady that the building was very unstable and there was a chance of another explosion.

"I don't care how unsafe it is, you will go in there now and get my Persian, she's very rare and highly expensive!" Mrs Whiting-Smythe was banging her fists on a table and her face was very red.

"I'm very sorry to hear your cat is still in there, but everyone else managed to collect their pet as they left the building."

"How dare you! I was in no fit state to pick up a heavy pet carrier, I have a weak back!"

The heated argument continued and it was obvious that nobody would be allowed back inside while the building was unsafe.

Bella was crying, she hated the idea of a cat being trapped and was upset that no-one was doing anything. Oscar couldn't bear to see Bella sad. He had a plan and crept away, back towards the hall. He was determined to find Snowdrop, even though he didn't like her much.

He crawled under the tape that was supposed to keep people out. The air was still thick with dust and he couldn't see a thing. He closed his eyes to keep the grit out and concentrated on his other senses to find his way round. He tried to remember where he had last seen her, and worked his way through the debris.

"Snowdrop? Snowdrop? where are you?"

He stopped to listen and heard a very quiet, weak whimper, more of a squeak than a meow. He cautiously edged round the corner of a fallen timber and saw the pet carrier caught underneath. Snowdrop was huddled towards the back, struggling for breath.

"Snowdrop, are you alright?" Oscar could only just make out a blur of white fur.

"Help me." Snowdrop's voice was unnaturally quiet, she sounded very weak and her breathing was uneven. "I'm bleeding and I can't move."

Oscar knew he had to act quickly. Another explosion would finish them both off, but he had no idea how to get Snowdrop out of the carrier safely.

"You look like you're in a bit of a pickle," Charlie appeared out of the murk and was rubbing his chin with his paw, taking in the problem.

Oscar was so pleased to see his friend, "I don't know what to do, Snowdrop is trapped and she's injured and…"
"Don't worry lad, there's always more than one solution to a problem. If we work as a team, we can do this," said Charlie calmly.

Charlie gave Oscar various instructions and he followed them like a soldier would his officer. He opened the latch on the pet carrier.

Inside Snowdrop was hardly recognisable. Her fur was covered in dust and matted blood. He gently nudged her with his nose, "Snowdrop you need to get up now, we need to get you out of the building, it's not safe to stay here."

Snowdrop was very weak, but managed to crawl out of the carrier. Oscar told her to climb onto his back as she couldn't walk.

With great care they made slow but steady progress through the rubble. Oscar felt like his back was breaking, Snowdrop really was quite heavy. The rubble and debris was painful to walk on, especially with the extra weight, but Oscar just kept focused on getting out. A chink of light was ahead, slicing through the gloom like a lighthouse. A few more steps and the three cats finally reached the security tape around the boundary.

"Oh my goodness! Mr Macintosh come quickly, we need your help quite urgently." Mrs Davis gently picked Snowball up off Oscar's back.

Mr Macintosh rubbed his eyes in disbelief. In all his years as a vet, he'd never seen anything quite like it.

Suddenly there was another loud *BOOM*, as the remainder of the hall collapsed. The cats had only just made it out in the nick of time.

"Well, I think you have been extremely lucky, that was a very narrow escape." Mr Macintosh turned his head to look at the pile of rubble that had been the Village Hall only an hour earlier. "I'm going to take Snowdrop back to my surgery and let Mrs Whiting-Smythe know what's happened."

The next morning Oscar was having a lie-in, when the doorbell rang. A few moments later Mr Martin appeared with Bella and following them was Mrs Davis from the pet shop.

"I hope you don't mind us calling unexpectedly, but I really wanted to give you these." Mrs Davis handed a bowl, a rosette and an envelope to Mr Martin.

"Oscar won first place in the "Catrobatics," but he also won something else."

Mrs Davis took a large silver trophy from her bag. It was engraved with Oscar's name and said "Best in Show".

"Of course, there's more to this story than meets the eye," said Mrs Davis. "Oscar will also be on the front page of the Gazette tomorrow!"

Bella and Mr Martin both looked confused. Mrs Davis explained how she had seen Oscar carrying Snowdrop out of the rubble moments before the building collapsed.

"My goodness," said Mr Martin, "Oscar you're very lucky to be here!"

Oscar rubbed his head against Mr Martin's arm and gave Bella an extra cuddle, just so they knew he hadn't got into danger to scare them.

Bella was very proud. "Oscar, you're a real hero." As she sat stroking him, she noticed a pronounced and wiry grey hair that wouldn't lie straight. Nine lives had now become two.

In his next adventure, local cats disappear without a trace, but Oscar plays detective and is hot on the case.

Chapter 8

Cat nap

It was a sunny day in May when Max leapt over the garden fence in a bit of a hurry.

"Oscar, is your mum in?" Max sounded urgent. "I need her assistance with something. Your mum is the best sniffer I've ever met and right now I could do with her help."

Oscar was intrigued, he had no idea what a 'sniffer' was but wanted to know more and ran back into the house to get her.

Sally came quickly.

"Max is everything OK? What's happened?" she looked very concerned.

"The Meow Code has been activated. The Dawson cats have all gone missing in mysterious circumstances."

"All three cats?"

"Yes, they were out in the garden this morning and when their owner called them in for their lunch, not one returned. I spoke to Deedles who lives next door and she said a man and woman had been hanging around. She heard something like struggling, lots of hissing and meowing. A car or van then sped off towards the ring road."

Sally looked very worried, "Do you have anything for me to get the trail going?"

Oscar sat wide-eyed listening, he knew the Dawson cats.

"Just the bedding really, if you follow me we can sneak in through the cat flap and hopefully you can pick up the trail from there."

Max leapt back over the fence and Sally followed. Oscar was curious as to what was going on, but also worried for the three cats. He didn't know them really well, but he did know that they weren't the sort of cats to wander off and not tell anyone. Oscar decided to follow and see if he could find out any more.

The Dawson house had a big garden, lots of shrubs and a small water feature by the patio. Sally and Max had already gone through the cat flap, so Oscar peeked through the window to see what they were doing. Sally had her head and nose buried in a big fleecy blanket in the utility room. When she emerged she looked very serious and came back into the garden. Oscar hid behind the wheelie bin and watched as his mum very carefully walked the length of the garden, her head up, sniffing the air.

"They were definitely here this morning Max. The trail ends very abruptly at the driveway. I think Deedles is right. Amber, Tiger and Smudge have been catnapped."

Oscar was shocked. Someone had taken the cats against their will and on purpose. Sally was always warning him and his sisters not to approach strangers.

"Sally, can you pick up a trail of the vehicle they were in? I'll send a meow message to warn other cats to keep indoors and if anyone has seen or heard anything to get in touch."

Max jumped onto the fence and then onto the garage roof of the house. He then proceeded to wail and howl in a way that Oscar didn't really understand. He could make out occasional words...*Update...Catnapped...Stay Inside...Danger...*Max's voice was very loud and powerful and carried right across the rooftops.

Then Oscar heard a reply, faint but audible...*Understood... Keeping Watch.* The cats communicated in a series of high-pitched wails at the beginning that seemed to signify the urgency of the message. The Meow Code was something his mum had talked about, but he had never heard it used before.

Sally walked into the street, her head still raised. Sniffing and stopping, stopping and sniffing.

"I'm certain that the vehicle is diesel not petrol. There's a slight hint of rust, so I'm guessing it's quite old. The man smokes cigars and sweats heavily. The woman wears a heavy, musky perfume and eats a lot of garlic." Sally was now poking her head in a nearby bush. "Here's a sandwich wrapper, it's the woman's and it was bought from the delicatessen in the village this morning." A discarded cigar butt nearby also confirmed the man had been there too.

Max looked thoughtful, "Good sniffing. You have another word with Deedles, see if she can remember anything else. I'll have a chat with Charlie and Sheba, see if they saw anything unusual earlier on today."

Oscar was still hiding behind the bin and waited until his Mum and Max had left the garden before he came out of his hiding place. He really wanted to help, but knew his Mum would say it was too dangerous.

He was thirsty so had a drink from the bottom basin of the water feature. It was really cold and tasted a bit strange, but he was hot so lapped it up. He found himself suddenly feeling very sleepy.

Oscar woke up and the first thing that struck him was he was moving and it was dark! He was in a cage with lots of other cats and was being wheeled across a courtyard to a windowless brick building. The moon hung in the sky like a large glowing globe, casting an eerie light on the cobbles.

They went into a shabby corridor and stopped at a door marked "LAB 7". As the door opened, the smell of chemicals was overpowering.

The room was filled with long, high metal tables, a number of deep sinks and various steel instruments were hanging from the walls. Along the far end of the wall were more cages and all were full of cats. Oscar guessed about sixty in total and as most were meowing, the noise was deafening.

"Will you lot shut up," Mary screeched over the noise. "You'll wake Trevor up and then you'll be sorry." She looked nervous, but opened the door and ushered the cats into another caged area. "I've put some tuna out for you, so hurry up and go inside."

Oscar was starving. He ran to the first bowl and started to eat. After a few mouthfuls though, he thought the tuna tasted strange. Nobody else noticed and all the cats were chomping on the fish with enthusiasm.

"I'd be careful of that if I were you," a white Persian sniffed the nearest empty bowl. "I wouldn't be surprised if they'd drugged the food as well."

Oscar instantly recognised the snooty tones of Snowdrop and recognised the taste in the food. It was the same weird taste as the water he'd drank from the fountain at the Dawson's house. The water that sent him to sleep and resulted in being catnapped!

He scanned the room again judging from the high barred

windows and heavy locked door, there was no escape. He felt hopelessness creep into his bones.

A movement towards the back of the room made him spin round quickly. One of the cats in the other cage had woken up and was now literally climbing the bars.

"Let me out of here!" She was meowing so loud the other cats had started to wake up too.

"What's all the noise?"

"Keep it down will you."

Oscar inched forward to get a better look at the vocal feline and got quite a shock. The cat was small, black and white with four white paws and tummy. It was like looking in a mirror, except she was a girl!

"Whoa, a copy cat." Oscar scrutinised his lookalike.

Snowdrop rolled her eyes in annoyance at the caterwauling.

"Will someone please shut her up, I'm getting a headache." The Persian sat down and put her paws over her ears.

"Shut up yourself," Molly pulled a face and meowed even louder.

"Well, I've never come across such rudeness."

"Ladies, ladies, bickering solves nothing." The Colonel was

a big brown cat and had placed a paw on Molly's shoulder to quieten her down. "We need a plan and we need to work together."

Oscar nodded his agreement, finally someone was talking sense. Colonel, Molly and the other cats had been there over a week and had witnessed something rather disturbing. A group of cats had been taken from the room yesterday and hadn't come back.

"Do you know why we've been taken?" Oscar wanted to find out as much information as he could. The Colonel relayed snippets of conversation he'd overheard between Mary and Trevor. The cats were being used for animal testing, an illegal practice but there was money to be made, so Trevor didn't care about breaking the law. Different chemicals were being applied to the skin, some scalded and burned like acid, others made all the fur drop out and the skin go scaly. Oscar shuddered. It sounded horrible. No wonder Molly was so keen to get out.

Oscar, Molly and The Colonel sat up all night trying to devise a foolproof plan, but try as they might, they couldn't think of how they could get out of the building. Oscar was getting agitated. He'd always managed to find a way out before and he was getting very frustrated as they kept reaching a dead end. Eventually, they all agreed that they would sleep on it and get their heads together in the morning.

It was eight o'clock in the morning and Trevor was in a foul mood. The last lot of experiments hadn't been successful.

The problem was, cat skin didn't react the same way to the chemicals as human skin and it was proving difficult to get hold of enough cats without arousing suspicion. He'd already seen a load of 'lost' posters in shop windows of owners desperate for the safe return of their beloved pet. Trevor had considered taking some of the "reward" cats back and claiming the money. In fact, the more he thought about it, the more he liked the idea. He stomped into the lab and thrust a sheet of paper in front of Mary. "I've had an idea of how we can make some money from this lot." He glared into Oscar's cage, who glared back at him.

Mary looked at the poster and saw a picture of a white Persian cat, sitting regally on a satin cushion. At the bottom of the picture it stated that there would be a reward of £1000 for the safe return of Snowdrop the Third.

Trevor had spotted Snowdrop at the back of the cage and was rubbing his hands at the thought of the reward.

Mary hesitated, "It's risky, but if you think it could work?" She didn't look completely convinced, but knew better than to contradict Trevor.

"Here's another one." He threw a handmade poster at her. "We'll start with these two and see how it goes. We'll take them back this afternoon".

Mary looked at the other poster, there was a picture of Oscar sat on Bella's knee. Bella had handwritten the poster.

MISSING CAT - OSCAR

My lovely cat Oscar is missing.

We all miss him very much and want him to come home safely.

If you have any information please get in touch

Thank you

Bella Martin, Sally, Sophie, Susie and Rocky xx

Mary put the two posters on a nearby bench and locked the door.

Snowdrop was the first to break the silence, "Well it appears I'll be going home after all." She looked around at the other cats. "It's a shame your owners didn't think highly enough of you to offer a reward too."

Oscar was furious. "That's not fair, don't be so mean! Not everyone can afford that kind of money."

"Yes, I notice your human didn't mention any. I'm surprised he's even considering taking you home without it being mentioned."

Oscar ignored Snowdrop, he had an idea. It was a long shot, but it could prove their only way of getting everyone out. He gathered all the cats around and explained how he thought it could be done. They all listened carefully and when he finished, the mood had brightened. Finally there was a glimmer of hope. Snowdrop didn't want to have any part in it at first, but Oscar curtly reminded her that if it hadn't been for him, she wouldn't be around to argue.

At 3.35 p.m Trevor and Mary came back to collect Snowdrop and Oscar.

"Right Mary, you're looking for the snooty white Persian and a black and white moggie with a smudge round his eye. He's the tester. If I don't get anything for him, I won't bother with the others that don't mention a reward."

At number 24 The Cedars, Mrs Whiting-Smythe had just handed over an envelope stuffed full of money to a man in a white van for the return of Snowdrop. She closed the door and picked up the Persian and noticed something very odd. Snowdrop the Third was wearing a dirty old black collar, not the pink diamante one she always wore. She inspected the metal disc and her brow furrowed in confusion. Who was The Colonel and why was Snowdrop wearing his collar? Unable to fathom it out, she rang the phone number inscribed on the back to see if they knew anything about it.

"Hello, Macintosh's Veterinary Practice, how can I help?"

Mrs Whiting-Smythe explained to the vet how Snowdrop had disappeared a week ago and had suddenly come home wearing the wrong collar.

Mr Macintosh listened intently and when she finished he said that his own cat, The Colonel, had also gone missing about a week ago too. In fact his waiting room was full of posters of missing cats and there had been sightings of a man and a woman in a white van acting suspiciously.

Mrs Whiting-Smythe felt all the colour drain from her face. She had just paid the very people who had stolen her cat in the first place!

It was 5.30pm exactly and Mr Martin had just arrived home from work when the doorbell rang. Bella answered it and a lady stood there who smelt of a mixture of musky perfume and garlic.

"Hello, I saw your poster for your lost cat and think I might have seen it."

Bella shrieked with delight, "Mum, Dad, come quickly."

Mrs Martin came in from the kitchen, a wooden spoon in her hand as she'd been busy stirring the gravy.

"What is it Bella? I'm busy making dinner"

"This lady says she's seen Oscar and she has the poster I made."

Mrs Martin looked at the nervous woman on the doorstep and didn't trust her one bit. Mary was screwing her hands up and resting on one foot and then the other. It was clear that something wasn't quite right.

"Do you have Oscar with you?" Mr Martin was now at the door looking towards the van and saw a man rummaging around in the back.

"Erm yes, maybe."

Mr Martin was suddenly suspicious and realised what this woman wanted.

"Obviously there'd be some sort of financial reward for your trouble," he said. The woman blushed and scurried back to the van. She returned with Trevor holding the cat carrier.

Mr Martin could see a small cat with black and white fur and the blue collar that they'd given Oscar that Christmas. He asked them to stand inside whilst he got his wallet. Bella couldn't wait to be reunited with Oscar, she flung open the carrier and scooped up the black and white cat.

"Dad, it's not Oscar!" Bella was confused. This other cat certainly looked a lot like Oscar, her colouring was almost identical, but she was lighter and her face was more feminine looking.

The man and woman were making a hasty exit for the front door.

"Not so fast!" Mr Martin stuck his foot out and tripped the man over and he fell in a heavy heap on the hall rug. The woman clearly didn't know whether to leave him or make a run for it.

Outside a car pulled up and two uniformed police officers

got out and very soon Trevor and Mary were in the police van in handcuffs.

"Dad, what about Oscar?" Bella's lip was trembling.

"I don't know Bella," Mr Martin sounded very sad. "We'll just have to wait."

In the morning, after a terrible night's sleep, Bella was woken by a white paw batting her cheek. The little black and white cat that looked like Oscar had slept in her room all night.

Mr and Mrs Martin were already up drinking tea in the kitchen when there was a knock at the door. A policeman was outside.

"Morning," he nodded to both Mr and Mrs Martin. "I wondered if this belonged to you?"

PC Reece started to smile as he brought a cat carrier from behind him revealing the real Oscar!

It was a huge celebration in the Martin house. Oscar was so happy to be home and to know that his plan had worked. When he gave Molly his collar, a part of him was worried no-one would realise it wasn't him. As though reading his thoughts, Molly appeared.

"Hi Oscar, we did it!" she said with excitement. "Your plan was so clever, we outwitted the bad guys and everyone is safe now thanks to you."

As Molly was a stray cat, the Martin's took her in to join their family and she fitted in perfectly. She asked Oscar about his strange grey wiry hairs and he explained that every time he lost a life, he gained a hair. He'd discovered another grey hair after their experience, as nine lives became one!

In his next adventure, Oscar becomes a Dad and now he has a son, are all his adventures done?

Chapter 9

Circle of life

Molly had been with the Martins almost six months and had happily settled into her new way of life. The arrival of spring had brought another surprise. Molly was carrying kittens and Oscar was very excited he would soon be a dad. Bella had lined a cardboard box with a fleecy blanket for Molly in preparation for the kittens' arrival.

Molly gave birth to three beautiful, healthy kittens, two girls and a boy. The little boy was the double of Oscar and the little girls were a smokier colour, looking like tiny little Sallys.

Bella adored the kittens and as the days passed, Mr and Mrs Martin realised there was no way they would be able to re-home them, the kittens were destined to stay. Bella got straight to work naming them. Suki was the smallest of the girls and loved everyone and everything, her name meant "beloved". Stella was Latin for "star" and the kittens loved nothing better than to sit on the window ledge each night and stare at the stars. And finally there was Socks. He had white socks on both front legs and liked to steal Bella's school socks from the laundry basket and hide them, so he seemed aptly named.

The weeks flew by and Suki, Stella and Socks were all growing bigger by the minute. They'd had lots of visitors and good well wishes. Bea visited most days as it was easy for her to fly up to the attic window. Oscar made sure the kittens realised that Bea was a friend and not to be chased after. Mr Woo popped over some nights on his way out hunting to see if he could catch anything for the kittens. Molly always thanked him, but said the kittens needed to learn to hunt for themselves.

One Saturday morning, Molly and the kittens were curled up asleep in the spare bedroom in the attic when Socks woke up suddenly. A branch had broken off a tree and the wind had picked it up. It had rapped on the window like it wanted to come in. He got up, had a stretch and wandered over to the window. He sat on the ledge and looked out across the rooftops. The trees were swaying and Mrs Martin's washing was on the line, billowing in the gusts. It really was a blowy day. He could see into next door's garden and watched the big brown rabbit for a while. His owner had built a great big hutch and Rusty loved to run up and down at high speed. The wind was whistling through the cage and Rusty's ears lifted with each gust.

Socks hadn't officially been outside yet though he'd sat by the open window in the kitchen and loved the smell of the fresh air with hints of others things all mixed up; cut grass, flowers, pine trees, the earthy smell of the compost heap. Socks didn't want to be inside on a day that looked so much fun, he wanted to explore. If he was quick, no-one would even know he was gone.

He crept carefully down the spiral staircase onto the floor below and into Bella's bedroom. She always opened her bedroom window on a morning to air the room and Socks knew this was his best chance of getting outside undetected. He jumped on the bed and as tempting as it was to snuggle up in the soft duvet and go to sleep again, he wanted to go outside even more.

The window was just above Bella's computer desk and quite easy to get to from her bed. He bounced up and down a few times and then jumped over. Easy! He pawed at the window. It was only open a crack and he needed a bit more space. He pressed his face against the pane, but it was really stiff. He pushed with all his strength, but it wasn't moving an inch. Socks was determined though and not about to give up without a fight. He looked around for something to help him.

Bella had an old teddy bear, big and soft and perfect to cushion a running shove. Socks dragged the bear by the ear and sat it against the windowpane. He didn't have much desk to run along and gather speed, but it was his best shot and he was going to take it.

"One, two, three."

Socks ran at the toy like a rugby player about to tackle an opponent. He hit the bear in the middle of the stomach and felt the window move slightly. He caught his breath and then tried again, charging at the toy with all his might. As he hit the bear, the window suddenly gave way altogether and swung wide open.

Socks didn't have time to slow down and before he knew what was happening, he toppled out of Bella's bedroom window!

He desperately tried to grasp onto something, but there was nothing to hold onto. He was falling and fast. He tried to get himself upright, ready for the impact and scared how much it would hurt. He was hurtling toward the garden, but before he could even let out a cry, he went feet-first into freezing cold water. He had landed in the fish pond! He banged his front paw hard on a rock and he was going all fuzzy as he spluttered and tried to catch his breath. The more he struggled, the faster he sank. The water enveloped him with a steely, cold grip.

The Koi carp in the pond were not at all happy about the intrusion. As Socks started to sink, the fish swam over to the other side to avoid him. They didn't like cats at the best of times, having heard stories that they ate fish, so tried to keep out of their way. Having a cat in their pond though was very unsettling and the younger fish were quite frightened. The oldest and biggest carp had been resting by the shadow of the lilies, when she felt the water tremor. She looked over and saw the other fish moving away rapidly from a strange flailing creature. Out of curiosity, she swam towards the disturbance to find out what was going on. When she saw Socks, she realised the little kitten was in real trouble.

Back in the house, Oscar was hunting high and low for Socks. Bella had come home for lunch and had opened a tin of sardines for the kittens as a treat. It was very unlike Socks not to be first in line for a fishy snack.

"Stella, have you seen your brother anywhere?" She was happily munching on the sardines and shook her head.

"Suki, when did you last see Socks?"

"I don't know Dad, he wasn't in the room when I woke up. I haven't seen him this morning."

Oscar went downstairs and checked in all the rooms again, Socks was nowhere to be seen. The kitchen door had a cat flap into the garden and all the kittens had been told they weren't to use it until they were older. Although Oscar was certain he would have heard if the cat flap had moved, he decided to poke his head outside, just to make sure.

Socks was sinking fast and although he was trying desperately to grasp onto something, he kept slipping and his head would go under the water again. The old carp had tried to swim underneath him to get him to the surface, but the kitten was sinking like a stone.

Oscar looked out of the cat flap and saw a lot of splashing coming from the pond, accompanied by some strange noises. He raced over and caught sight of a small black and white head disappearing under the water. Without thinking, he jumped straight in. The pond was full of water lilies and the reeds were getting tangled in his paws, but Oscar knew he was Socks' only chance. He allowed himself to be engulfed by the water and then spotted Socks. With expert precision, he grabbed the kitten by the scruff of his neck. With all his might, Oscar dragged himself and Socks to the side of the pond.

Socks and Oscar were both spluttering and gasping for breath when Sally came out to see what all the commotion was about.

"Oscar! Socks! What on earth have you been doing? How did you end up in the pond? Don't you realise how dangerous the water is?"

Sally was a mixture of glad, sad and angry. Glad they were both safe, sad as Socks' paw was bleeding badly where he'd hit it on the rock and angry he'd put himself and Oscar in danger.

"I'm sorry," Socks spluttered. "I just wanted to have an adventure and it looked so much fun outside!"

Sally looked to Oscar and said, "I think you need to have a talk to Socks about the importance of looking after his lives."

"Grandma Sally has a point Socks. What you just did was very silly and dangerous, you could have drowned."

"I know Dad, I didn't mean to get into trouble." Socks looked so forlorn that Oscar couldn't stay angry at him for long.

"You had a very narrow escape and were lucky I was around to fish you out. I can't blame you for wanting to explore, but next time come and see me and we'll do it together! Grandma Sally has a saying 'Four paws in the air, don't go there, four paws on the ground, safe and sound!' It's very good advice."

He gave his son an affectionate pat on the head and that's when he noticed it. Socks' first grey wiry hair that refused to lie flat.

THE END

About Sara Fellows

Sara has been telling stories since she was a young girl and would happily spend hours entertaining her friends and family with tales she'd dreamt up.

When writing stories, she starts with the glimmer of an idea and follows the direction her imagination takes her. *The nine lives of Oscar the cat* is Sara's first novel and was inspired by her own cat and his mischievous ways.